PRAISE FOR BRITTA JENSEN

"Hirana's War is a wondrously beautiful conclusion to the *Eloia Born* duology. The sweeping worldbuilding and adventure will leave you breathless. Britta Jensen captures the fragility of coming of age and Leanora's strength and resilience in choosing to stand against the odds."

— AR BENNETT, AUTHOR

"A coming of age, teen angst, magical teen saves world, love story set on a remote planet but oh the world building in this book!"

— YALONDA WILHOITE, MIDDLE SCHOOL TEACHER

"An incredibly thought-provoking and intriguing concept: the use of music to fly, to heal, to transport across worlds, and even as a weapon."

— TARA LUNDMARK, AUTHOR

I0587927

GHOSTS OF YOKOSUKA

A SHORT STORY

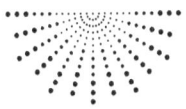

BRITTA JENSEN

First published in the United States in 2021 by Murasaki
Press LLC
Copyright © 2021 by Britta Jensen
Cover design by Stuart Bache

*All characters and events in this publication, other than those
clearly in the public domain, are fictitious and any resemblance to
real persons, living or dead, is purely coincidental.*

Murasaki Press supports the value of copyright and the
right of every artist to be compensated for their work. The
scanning, uploading, and distribution of this book without
permission is a theft of the author's intellectual property. If
you would like permission to use material from the book
(other than for review purposes), please contact info@
murasakipress.com. Thank you for your support of author's
rights.

Murasaki Press LLC
PO Box 152313
Austin, TX 78715
U.S.A.
Join the author's mailing list at www.britta-jensen.com

The book has been catalogued for libraries as follows:
Names: Jensen, Britta, author.
Title: Ghosts of Yokosuka / Britta Jensen.
Description: Austin, TX : Murasaki Press, 2021. | Summary:
Fourteen-year-old Annabelle's only friends are ghosts until
Jake turns up in Yokosuka, Japan, and sets her life on a new
path. | Audience: Grades 7 & up.
Identifiers: ISBN 978-1-7363835-2-0 (paperback) | ISBN
978-1-7363835-1-3 (ebook) | ISBN 978-1-7363835-3-7
(audiobook)
Subjects: LCSH: Family life--Fiction. | Ghosts--Fiction. |
Japan--Fiction. | Bildungsromans. | Young adult fiction. |
Fantasy fiction. | BISAC: YOUNG ADULT FICTION /
Fantasy / General. | YOUNG ADULT FICTION / Family /
General. | YOUNG ADULT FICTION / Coming of Age. |
GSAFD: Bildungsromans. | Fantasy fiction.
Classification: LCC PZ7.1.J46 Gh 2020 (print) | LCC
PZ7.1.J46 (ebook) | DDC [Fic]--dc23.

ALSO BY BRITTA JENSEN

Novels

Eloia Born

Hirana's War

Short Stories

Three Fingers

First Noel

The Coral Ring

For Sarah, Cynthia and Fatima who have helped dispel lingering, unwanted ghosts.

CHAPTER ONE

My only friends were ghosts. I was so accustomed to their floating spirits around me that I wasn't certain I could trust real humans with my feelings. Koji, a chubby child spirit, bobbed in and out of the crowd of hundreds waiting in the August Japanese heat. I followed him away from where my mom and brother stood on the crowded pier. *Would it always be like this?* I had wanted to ask Koji. It was 1985 and Yokosuka's bustle surrounded the naval ships' arrivals and departures. My ghosts always perked up when they got word the ships were coming in, like their lives were so boring always following me around.

"Annabelle, give me lumpia," Koji whined. "*Hara heta.* I'm hungry." He floated up and down beside me, fat arms crossed.

"You can't eat it." I whispered softly, keeping the basket of my Mom's freshly made lumpia away from him.

"Please…" he pleaded loudly in my ear.

Mom waved me over to join her under her

white sun parasol. Heaven forbid my naturally brown skin should get darker. I hadn't allowed her to slather any whitening cream on me, so I tucked unwillingly underneath, Koji following behind. We had been waiting on the pier for the USS Ranger since early that morning. The noontime heat of the concrete was melting the bottoms of my flip-flops. I turned my back on the sun to face the verdant hillside where the cicadas alternated between a cack-a-lack buzzing and a hissing sound that wore on my patience.

"So hungry," Koji whined.

"Shut up," I said.

"Who are you talking to?" Mom asked, eyes trained on the deep blue ocean before us, ignoring my brother whispering to himself.

"No one," I said.

The throng of women and children pressed into me, knocking our little family back against a concrete pylon. Just around the bend in the harbour, an aircraft carrier's bow came into view. I craned my neck and spotted a teenage boy standing alone. Unlike us, he had a small bit of space around him. I hadn't seen him at school and pale kids like him were a rarity. He pushed through an enormous family setting up banners to stand a few feet away from us. His eyes felt older and sadder than the rest of him. Freckles threatened to take over his flushed cheeks and unsmiling mouth. He was somewhere between my age, fourteen, and a young fifteen. I hoped he would shift his gaze toward the approaching ship so I could get a better look at him.

"Another ship, another day." Widow, my other ghost friend, floated above us, her gaze settling on my mother's heavily hair sprayed bangs. Her blatant dislike of Mom made me grin.

The sound of the boat's horns brought my attention back to the aircraft carrier's tugboats straining to guide the behemoth into the dock. The ship was hours behind schedule, which I was learning was normal for the U.S. Navy. My parents had only been married a year and a half, but two cruises had taught me the subtle difference between a disappearing yakuza birth-father and a sailor stepfather.

"Purse, Rocky!" Mom said to my seven-year-old brother, still rocking in place, ignoring her.

My mom's make-up smeared in the thick humidity and she fanned herself before I unhooked her purse from Rocky's shoulder so she could reapply her fuschia lipstick and powder.

"Less lipstick next time," Widow whispered to Mom, though she couldn't hear her.

The countryside of Cebu had trained my mother early to love creams that bleached her skin to hide her "Filipino" half. Her father was an American GI whose only advice in the three years she'd known him had been to get off the island the first chance she got. At sixteen she'd left for Japan with only her mother's secret recipe for lumpia and her hazel eyes as a reference for her new life here. It didn't take long for the underworld and my yakuza birthfather to claim her. Once she'd met my stepfather, Duke, she wasn't about to go back to where we came from—if she had a chance at something better on the coveted, but microscopic naval base. Duke represented something more than love: free healthcare, bullying-free school, and a chance for her children to speak perfect American English. I'd seen how she'd thrown everything that she had at Duke, like he could carry her away from dive bars and Yokosuka's "special price" *gaijin* premium rents.

I had promised myself I would never be so desperate to catch a man. Yet, here I was trying to get a glimpse of the boy with the sad eyes again, but he'd moved. Rocky grabbed the basket of lumpia out of my hand. I was temporarily knocked off balance and crashed into someone. A solitary lumpia rolled next to my foot where Rocky scooped it up and devoured it.

"Rocky, it's dirty, no..." I tripped over my brother and fell.

"I would have done the same." The boy with sad eyes stood over me. He helped me off the burning wharf and I offered him a fragrant lumpia and he quickly ate it in two bites. Mom said the secret was to add a touch of curry powder.

He was looking at me like he expected a response. I needed to find the right words, make sure I spoke English. Instead, I stared at the silver charm bracelet on his wrist.

The past year I had been very good at saying the wrong things and remained friendless: not Filipino enough for the Pinoy crowd, nor Japanese enough for the half-Japanese kids. I was half the wrong combinations. It did not help that my eyes were two slightly different shades of hazel and brown. Forget hanging with the proper Americans, they had their own problems. It was still better than being a pariah, like I'd been all my previous years at Yokosuka Chugaku, the local city school. Half-Japanese-anything kids were the targets for all sorts of torture.

How did I start a conversation without explaining any of this? Rocky stole another lumpia from the basket and my mother was about to scold me when she saw the boy. She stared at his ill-fitting clothes. Mom lived in a world of dolls: her reality rarely touching mine. In spite of the heat, she wore platform heels, nylons and a candy pink long stocking dress. In my sailor dress, already eschewing anything saccharine, I was a disappointment to her.

When Rocky spotted the Super Mario Brothers logo on the boy's tight t-shirt, he went berserk. "You like Mario Brother?" He didn't wait for a response and grabbed the logo on the t-shirt. "Luigi my favourite."

An internal, burning heat spread from my face down my neck. Rocky was unaware he could have ruined any chance at making my first friend. Because he never acted like he needed friends he figured I was in the same boat: destined to wander the world as alone and yet fully occupied in my own world of ghosts as he was in his made-up world. I looked at Widow and Koji floating ahead of us. Since it was summer vacation there was still a chance the new boy would forget the encounter.

"Annabelle like Luigi too," Rocky said in his prematurely low voice.

He would definitely remember us now.

"I'm Jake." He held out his hand, then retracted it to wipe a greasy palm on his orange shorts before shaking Rocky's hand.

"I'm Annabelle." I shook his hand, unsure how long to hold it before retracting.

Rocky hugged him, surprising Jake. I was certain he'd run away, but Jake smiled at me, those sad green eyes crinkling. I had to look away because Koji was making a stupid face behind him.

"You like him!" Koji sang, his pudgy face contorting. "I'm telling."

"Tell me what?" Widow chased him through the crowd, providing temporary relief from his teasing.

"Want more lumpia?" I asked, making sure to ignore Mom's gaze.

Cheers went up as the aircraft carrier came alongside the pier and the crowd pushed us closer together. Jake smelled like fabric softener. Everyone was swarming to glimpse the sailors manning the rail in their summer whites.

"Why you alone?" Mom asked.

"My mom's not here and my dad's on that ship." Jake met my mom's questions without embarrassment, his gaze even and steady.

He didn't notice her staring at the girl's charm bracelet he wore when she thought he wasn't looking. Widow floated in front of the approaching carrier that eclipsed the unforgiving Japanese sun. I lifted my burning feet, trying to find balance. Jake put his hand on my elbow to steady me, a rush of warmth flooding my limbs.

Act normal, I told myself.

The crowd surged forward and one family belted "I'm proud to be an American." They were too off-key to be cute.

"Your Dad works below deck?" Jake asked.

"Step-dad. No, he's on the flight deck." I replied. "Yours?"

"Engineering." Jake replied.

My mom grinned knowingly. I needed her to go away. Widow bobbed above the rail, watching the departing sailors, like she did every time a ship came into port. She was searching for her dead husband, despite his having disappeared forty-four years ago during a sea battle in the middle of World War II. According to Koji, she'd poisoned herself in the hopes her wandering soul could be reunited with her husband.

Yokosuka City, the only place I'd ever known, glittered in the afternoon sun as the red Keihin Kyuko train steamed through the middle of the city, its electric motors making a saxophone sound before zooming south. Jake watched the train with interest. I wanted to say something interesting, but I had no idea how to communicate with anyone my age.

The crowd of hundreds had thinned to a few stragglers perched on the pylons. A man in blue dungarees called out to us, holding a clipboard.

"Jake Sturgess?" he asked, lifting an envelope off the clipboard.

"That's me." Jake took the envelope, but didn't open it.

"Your Dad's still in hospital in Indonesia. He has to stay until the Doc clears him." The sailor looked back at his clipboard. "Everything you need should be there. I'll leave you to the care of these good folks." He clapped a hand on Jake and disappeared up the gangway.

I looked at Jake's flushed cheeks, how he turned the envelope over and over, and looked back at the ship. I knew that feeling, without knowing how to name it.

"Where are you stay—" my question was interrupted by a glimpse of my stepfather locked in a clingy embrace with Mom, noisily kissing her. After a six-month separation I knew it was time to leave them to it.

Jake had taken off, walking in long, loping strides toward the tunnels that lead away from the pier.

"Wait!" I said.

He stopped, still clutching the envelope. Widow floated over him.

Rocky tugged on me, holding up 3,000 yen. Bribery courtesy of my mother. It was enough money for three days of food and public transportation. The only missing thing was a note stating: "Dear children: stay far, far away until I'm ready for you to clean the house."

I snatched the money away, calling out to Jake. "Ready for an adventure?" I started to tremble a little from nerves, but maintained eye contact.

Jake walked forward gingerly. "What do you have in mind?"

"Let's get off-base."

Rocky roared in approval, motoring around. I didn't like the idea of him tagging along and ruining everything. It was hard enough with Widow and Koji constantly offering commentary, not to mention their occasional friend ghosts sometimes joining in the bizarre spectacle that was my life.

"Finally." Koji reappeared and followed Rocky on his circuit.

"We could take my bike. I've got pegs you can ride on." Jake offered.

I looked between him and Rocky. If we took Jake's bike, we could get to the train station faster, but it meant leaving Rocky behind. My brother ran circles around my mom and step-dad, who were blissfully snogging. Rocky had been a constant weight on my life, but could I abandon him?

I was aware of the dangers awaiting him

without proper supervision. Mom's appetite for temper tantrums was the least of his worries. But, at some point she had to grow up. If I didn't take a small taste of freedom now, when would I? What was the worst that could happen? I tried to imagine that, but my fourteen-year-old brain couldn't think beyond the present.

"Let's go. Now!" I ran with Jake toward the front gate, leaving the basket behind. We darted toward the bike racks. I kept listening for the drone of my mother's accented English, anything to indicate that my adventure was grinding to a halt. The only sounds were the cars and clamor of sailors departing the base. Jake wrapped his bike lock around the tree and fastened it before attaching the key to his charm bracelet. He mounted his bike and put one hand out to steady me while I stood on the pegs. "Hold onto me." I gripped his shoulders and we surged forward. It was my first time touching a boy my age. Ever. I was afraid to grip too hard, to touch him in the wrong way. I had read about encounters like this in my manga, but to feel the muscle and bone, the pulsing of his shoulders as he ped-alled—it was different from what I imagined. I had to keep a firm grip or I'd go flying off. I'd heard American boys didn't like wimpy girls.

"No riding on pegs! You have to walk through the gate!" The Marines bellowed at us in their dress blues while we rushed under the front gate's awning. Koji and Widow floated behind us, a new jubilance in their faces.

"This way." I pulled at his shirt to steer us away from the Chuo District and toward the JR Railway at the north end of my city. Jake slowed down, craning his neck to look up at the signs in my city that had felt mundane: the same grocer, yarn and embroidery, and stationers' shops that had always been there. His questions were non-stop:

"What did that sign mean?"

"Why does it smell like fish?"

"Are those displays of real or fake food?"

I had lived my entire life in Yokosuka, so I relished seeing it through his new eyes. The pancake stand seller called out to us "*Irashyaimase!*" There was a new twang in his weather-beaten voice. I held on gently to Jake's shoulders as we arrived on the other side of the bay. I hopped off when we pulled into the station's circular drive.

"Where are we going?" he asked.

"Kamakura, where the good beaches are." I dared hold his gaze. "It's the best, you'll see." I was surprised at the boldness in my voice.

He looked much calmer once we dismounted. "Can I bring my bike on the train?"

I looked over at the ticket taker snoozing over the money plate. "If we're quiet, we can leave our ticket stubs with him and sneak through."

Jake handed me a 1,000 yen bill and I purchased both our tickets.

"I'll pay you back." I said. "When we go to the *konbini*."

"The what?" he asked.

"It's like a little shop with all the small things you need. They're everywhere and have the best snacks."

He glanced behind me at the Tokyo bay sparkling as a blue JR train pulled into the station. Unlike the smooth-sounding Keihin Kyuko trains, this one bumped and squealed with age. We boarded and found two seats. His gaze drifted to the advertisements for escort services and travel shops fluttering from the air-conditioning fan in the middle of the train. The soft, velvet blue seats cushioned my aching limbs. He sat closer to me than I'd expected, his arms settling next to mine. I could see where the dark hairs on his arm had been bleached at the top from the sun.

"Have you been outside the base much?" I asked.

An old woman stared and whispered in contempt at us before moving several seats over. This was fairly usual for foreigners. If I didn't open my mouth and my hair covered my face, sometimes I could pass as Japanese, but never for long. Koji and Widow followed the nasty old woman and made faces that I ignored, though I was secretly pleased with their loyalty. If I encouraged them, they'd only make me laugh and I didn't need Jake thinking I was a lunatic.

"It's my first time leaving the base since I arrived a few months ago," he said.

I couldn't imagine what would keep him on the tiny compound until he fiddled with his charm bracelet.

"It was my Mom's. It's the only thing I was allowed to keep, except her books, after she died," he said.

"I'm sorry, I didn't mean to stare."

A warning beep sounded before the train doors closed and we were moving along the bumpy old track. My words were failing me. I wanted to take his mind off whatever was causing his face to pull taut from holding all the emotion just below the surface of his skin. I knew that feeling.

"Kamakura is my favourite place. Everything there is hundreds, sometimes thousands of years old."

Jake kept his gaze fixed outside the window. "Thanks for doing this. I'm already having more fun these last few minutes than I've had in a month of living here." He looked at me, smiled, then watched the landscape change as we travelled away from the city through darkened tunnels and toward the opposite shore. Ancient stone temples and crimson *torii* gates led the way up to hillside shrines tucked into thick, green foliage.

WHEN WE ARRIVED INTO THE KAMAKURA MAIN station, groups of teens in indigo *hakama* passed by carrying golden shrines on wooden pegs. A throng followed calling out chants, while *ika* barbecue wafted over us, and my stomach prickled with hunger.

"What's that for?" Jake asked, pointing at the teens.

"To honor their dead ancestors. It's O Bon season. Kamakura is one of the spiritual centers of this area. At least, that's what my dad used to say before he left us."

Koji and Widow reappeared and hovered on either side of me.

"Go away." I whispered. How could I get to know him with them around?

"No chance," Widow said, a soft smile playing on her lips, a glow in her black eyes.

Jake mounted his bike, waiting for me. It was the first time I wanted my ghosts to truly disappear. They had been my pseudo protectors from bullies and yet in a moment like this, they felt like a detractor from a semi-normal outing. I climbed on the pegs willing myself to ignore them as we zipped past the Enoden streetcar hissing along its narrow tracks. The conductor called out the stops in a reedy voice.

"Why does everyone talk through their noses here?" Jake asked.

"I guess it's like talking in our throats in English," I replied.

I hadn't noticed anything nasal about Japanese until he pointed it out. It was a language, like English, I'd spoken my whole life. I'd always assumed a higher pitched voice in Japanese meant you were friendlier. I had often used this "friendly voice" to get my mom out of scrapes when she took over my dad's bar. My father had always spoken Japanese in a low-throated voice that had frightened me, especially in rare moments when he corrected my speech. "Can't speak like a half-breed. Already have a strike against you." He'd point at my light eyes, like he wasn't part of the problem.

I didn't want to think about my dad. I held on tighter to Jake's shoulder as he picked up speed. The stretch of beach near Enoshima had a *konbini* with the freshest snacks. I bought us a few onigiri and melon drinks there. The late afternoon sun seemed less oppressive when we came out of the freezing store. Ahead of us, a boulder stuck out of the ocean with an orange *torii* gate on top of it. Enoshima jutted out from the beach like a tiny whale with a long, thin tongue connecting it to the mainland. I searched the low tide in the distance to find something to say. "We can leave your bike here by the rocks."

We took off our shoes, the warm sand cushioning our feet until we found a spot that was free of debris and food litter. I dug out an onigiri with tuna in the middle and handed the meat one to Jake, the plastic covering already sweating in the late afternoon heat. He peeled off the outer wrapping and instead of cringing over eating seaweed, he ate all of it.

I didn't expect that he would eat Japanese food so normally. Usually my American classmates disliked seaweed. I looked out to the sea, trying to act like it was normal for me to take cute boys I didn't know to the beach. I had to relax, which was why I brought him here. Everyone liked the ocean. They had to. The roar of it against the waves meant I wouldn't have to provide conversation. There was enough to look at, to do. This was where I took Rocky when I needed a day away from the house and an easy place to babysit him.

Koji and Widow walked along the beach, conversing noisily in English. They sounded so stupid, pretending to have this deep conversation and stopping periodically to see if I was watching them. They were worse than Rocky trying to act like he wasn't up to something.

"My mom would have loved it here," Jake said, laying back on his elbows and stretching out his feet in the warm sand.

"What happened to her?" I felt like it was better to know instead of dancing around it. I kept my gaze trained on the small waves and listless surfers past the breakers.

"Cancer. It was really fast. My dad was still out to sea, so I had to come here and stay with his division buddy's family."

"I'm sorry…it must be so… *taihen* …hard," I said.

Would my life with my family have been better if my birthfather died instead of disappearing?

"I think everybody's family has something. Like your brother, he's funny, but I bet he's a handful," Jake said.

"Nothing is easy with him." I watched Jake's face, to gauge whether to keep talking. He didn't look away. "Rocky used to go to a special school. Except, he kept getting lost on the train. My mom and I tried everything to help him get to school by himself." There. It was out. Would he feel differently about me now?

His face didn't change, his eyes meeting mine. His green irises picked up the glints of the afternoon sun, reflecting yellow flecks. My vision settled lower on his mouth, then roved back to his steady gaze. So much eye contact felt uncomfortable and I had to look away.

"Isn't he too young to take the train?" he asked.

"It's normal for young kids here. Rocky can take the train by himself when he wants to get somewhere. But, instead on school days he'd go fishing or swimming instead. Before we moved to the base, an old man brought him to the police station."

Koji dove in the water ahead, breaking my concentration.

"What did your mom do?"

"I lied and said my mom was in the hospital. I had to pick him up from the police station."

"She shouldn't have let you do that," Jake leaned in, his face clouding.

"She can't really speak Japanese. At least not..." I couldn't tell him about the bar and how her vocabulary extended as far as telling people prices and giving them change. A little small talk here and there, some memorized jokes. Before my birth-father left I hadn't noticed her pidgin Japanese. I suppose because he was usually there, drinking with his buddies, making deals my Mom didn't understand. As long as she kept acting like the doll that my father thought he'd owned, everything was *daijobu*, okay.

He sat there for a while, neither of us speaking, a weight in both of us we didn't have the words for. Widow floated above the water, her kimono changing from a light pink back to her everyday light grey. She sang a slow tune and Jake craned his head.

"Is someone singing nearby?"

I didn't know what to say. There was no way anyone could hear them, at least I hadn't experienced that for years and it took everything Widow, Koji and one of their friends did to make an appearance at an opportune time at the school girl's bathroom years ago. It was best to go along with him, acknowledge there was music but not tell him about them. He'd freak out for sure. "Yeah, somewhere...you want to go swimming?"

"We don't have swim suits," he looked puzzled.

"Doesn't matter." It was nearly sunset and the beach was fairly empty. I quickly threw my dress over my head, keeping my slip on and waded into the soupy water, which calmed my nerves.

Jake peeled off his red t-shirt and dove into the water after me. A purple-blue mass glowed below the surface. Jelly fish blimped about a few meters beyond where Jake swam.

"What are those?" He asked.

"Jellyfish. Don't worry, the sting feels like a tiny rubberband."

He splashed away, terrified.

The air around the glowing jellyfish changed and an enormous grin rose out of the water, following by Koji holding a sword. "Ah, Anna-chan! More fun with no Rocky!" He raised his sword and tried to stab at the jellyfish, which floated about undeterred.

"What was that?" Jake asked. He faced Koji who stopped stabbing, a look of guilt on his face.

"Don't ruin my time with him," I whispered to Koji.

"Did you say something?" Jake asked, wading back to shore.

"Just talking to myself." I said, then wished I hadn't.

Jake walked back to our stuff and rifled through the bag of food, guzzling one of the drinks before stopping, a sour look on his face. "What is this?"

"It's melon drink," I called out. "It's really good."

His face said otherwise as he squinted.

I swam toward him, standing when I felt my knees crunch against the particulate of the sand. The sudden drag of gravity on my body after swimming made me want to retreat back into the sea. The sun was sinking below the horizon. I wanted to stay there, in the cooling sand until the moon came up, but the mosquitos would come out soon and it was best to show Jake more of Kamakura.

"Let's see Hachimangu shrine. It's at the center of Kamakura," I said to Jake. The later I stayed out, the longer I could pretend that my mother wouldn't be upset I'd left Rocky with her. Koji drew his sword in the air and whirled off. Widow floated beside me.

We got dressed in our sandy clothes, trying to shake out as many of the irritating grains as possible. I climbed on his bike, his shoulders a little more familiar as I came closer, leaning into the motion of him soaring forward. I felt impenetrable from the people staring and pointing at us. That was a first.

"Which way?" He asked.

"Follow the street car tracks back to the city center," I said.

HACHIMANGU SHRINE WAS BATHED IN YELLOW light, a series of torii gates leading up to the temple. It's black and white awning curved up and around its two red and orange *oni* guardians. We left his bike at the temple gates and walked along the cobblestone path surrounding the complex. I basked in the wonder in Jake's appreciative face. A long line of women dressed in bright indigo yukata trotted by, fanning themselves.

"Where are they going?" he asked following behind them.

Drums sounded from the hillside, echoing across the valley. During O Bon season it made sense. It had been a long time since I'd been able to participate in O Bon, back before my father left.

"Let's see," I took his sleeve and directed him to the stone steps.

The taiko drums trilled again, then pounded in a steady bass rhythm and we followed them up the hillside, the aroma of barbecued chicken prickling our nostrils. Enka music broadcast over a crackling loudspeaker, a woman crooning about the moon.

Tsuki ga, detta detta, tsuki ga ta yoi, yoi.

The music reminded me of my father drinking sake and imitating the throaty music on nights when the bar had made enough to clear his gambling debts. He had been a good singer.

When we rounded the curve in the foliage, a dirt playground opened up to a square stage set in the middle. Over a hundred people were arranged in rings circling the stage with four dancers demonstrating around the taiko drummers. The music reverberated inside me, the familiar dance making me sway. I couldn't ignore the deep, inner tug and I immediately joined the dance. Jake watched me from the side lines, the ghosts settling above him.

My hands swayed automatically with the music I'd known since childhood. My arms swooped in and out with the movements of the other dancers. I was transformed from something in-between to feeling rooted to the dirt circle I danced upon. I was no longer Annabelle, the "ghost girl" with no friends. I was someone graceful and lithe, creating cranes and flowers with my floating limbs, stepping in time with the taiko's rhythm.

The music came to a stop, the loudspeaker hissing.

"What are those?" Jake asked, pointed above us.

My ghosts were dancing with each other. The song continued above, Koji playing the shakuhachi and Widow singing along.

I was half terrified. Would I lose him, if he knew? What explanation could I come up with that would keep him from making fun of me? "What do you see?"

"A woman...a child?" He followed their movements, his face ashen. "Am I hallucinating?" His hand traced their dance across the sky.

"They're my ghosts." I said and watched him carefully. He didn't make any eye contact, his body very still. I exhaled a tension I'd held onto for years. "They've been my companions since forever."

"Oh." He looked up again, crossing his arms in front of him protectively. A few moments passed of him watching them, before his arms settled at his side, his body visibly relaxing. "Wow. I can't believe I'm seeing them." He beamed at me. "You're really lucky." Color returned to his face and I felt a tightness in my stomach unclench, if only a little.

"Are there always only two of them?" He asked.

"Usually. Sometimes they bring friends, but only for special occasions."

He hadn't run away. That had to be something. I sighed, afraid to look up at him again, to see if he had changed his mind about the weird person I was and now couldn't pretend to be otherwise.

The crowd milled about, staring at us speaking English and looking up at the starless sky. Widow stopped singing, bowed to Koji, and he flicked his fan at her before she dashed off, blowing sparks on him.

"*Oyasuminasai!*" Koji streaked off in a blue trail.

Jake was standing so close to me I could see the perspiration drops on his nose. I took out my handkerchief to wipe them off, but he gingerly took my hand, using his other hand to dab at his face with the handkerchief before placing it in his back pocket.

"I wish they'd show me my mom one last time." His hand was warm and dry.

"I wish they had that power," I squeezed his palm gently, trying to appear calm when it felt like all the nerve fibers on my hand were increasing the blood supply to my heart.

The red lanterns above us glowed differently than any other lanterns I'd ever seen. I wished my ghosts could slow everything down so I didn't have to go home. When the music started again, Jake followed, dancing behind me, like it was nothing to dance to music he'd never heard before and didn't understand. I was afraid of the new sound of my heart beating in my ears, a soft voice telling me that things were changing.

CHAPTER TWO

When we arrived back in Yokosuka, the lights from across the Tokyo bay flickered at us. We were both stalling. The aroma of fresh crepes at the sidewalk stands gave us another excuse to stay out longer. I let go of his hand to buy a banana-choco crepe. It was warm, some of the chocolate syrup gushing out when Jake leaned in to take a bite. His pale skin reflected the lights of the shopping plaza shutting down for the night, a pedicab driver's lights whirling around him as he zoomed off.

What would it be like to be him? To not exist in this in-between world that I'd always lived in. I wondered, at that moment, if escape was my only option and if he, like some character in one of the mangas I'd stolen from *gomi* piles, would be willing to join me?

Or, did such things only exist in the realm of fantasy? Did I dare hope?

The sea lapped against the concrete jacks

that surrounded the bayside of the shopping plaza.

"I suppose we should head home, won't the family you're staying with worry about you?" I asked.

He shrugged, squinting as he looked upward before following me, his hand slipping into mine. "I don't think they'd notice that much. They have two little ones running around making problems all the time." He paused, his voice dropping, "Honestly, I like the break from the yelling. And all the beer I'm sure her husband is drinking." There was more, I could feel it in his voice.

I wanted to rescue him from that place, but my home wasn't any better. I didn't have the right to rescue anyone if I couldn't save myself from the whirling mess of my family.

We were within a few steps of the front gate of the naval base and I stopped, looking at all the women in their garish make-up and permed hair. Half of them looked a bit like my mom, with some variations for height and skin colour. There were a few Russian women. Most waved at the sailors as they walked by, not openly soliciting, but also not shying away from the guys who approached them, eventually sauntering together across the wide crosswalk that led into the inner workings of "the Honch" as Duke liked to call the string of bars that used to be my old home.

I spotted my mom waiting for us at the front gate of the base. She was pacing back and forth until she saw us and darted forward.

"Ship call Duke about Jake. Some message about his dad and I not know where you are." Alcohol fumes wafted off her and I stepped back.

"I was showing Jake Kamakura, like you said I should." She'd had enough to drink that it was possible she believed me.

Jake let go of my hand and slipped his charm bracelet onto my wrist. The sea breeze blew his sandy hair around. "It looks better on you." He turned my wrist so the charms caught the street light's reflection. "Thank you for today."

I leaned in closer to him and I could see my shadow reflected in his eyes. My mom pulled us apart, marching me up the hill, back to the base housing towers with their Bauhaus thickness that looked so out of place with the architecture of the rest of the city.

I STARED BLEARY-EYED AT THE PILE OF DISHES, cartons of take-out crowding the sink. I didn't understand how the three of them couldn't just throw things away. Why it had to be my job. Rocky puttered by, yellow blanket wrapped around him, despite the fact it was after midnight and he usually dropped off right at 9:00pm so that he could wake up at 7:00am without fail, every day.

"There's some yakisoba in the fridge I saved for you," Rocky said, biting his nubby nails. His brown eyes were piercing in the kitchen's fluorescent glow. "You take me with you tomorrow?" He asked, his voice husky.

"I don't know. You left me a mess here to clean up," I said. Then I felt bad. It wasn't his fault our parents were slobs.

"I help. I'll go get stool."

That was going to make a racket so I pulled it over next to the sink for him. A make-shift foldable table was set-up next to the countertops. Because my stepdad was low ranking the tower housing authorities hadn't bothered finishing the rest of the countertops adjoining the sink, so it required an extra table, though their heights were mismatched. Rocky climbed up the ladder, tying his blanket around his shoulders like a cape. The air conditioning made goose bumps rise on our arms.

"Garbage first," I said and he took the cartons of take-out and tossed them in the blue trashcan. He scurried up the ladder as I scrubbed each dish and handed it to him to rinse and place in the drying rack on the portable table. It felt like every surface of the kitchen was covered either in dishes or glasses. I had heard that we could get a dishwasher that hooked up to the sink, but my mother had complained it would take up too much room and get in the way of the women who came to her to get their hair washed and set for the week.

I'd watched them come in with greasy, limp hair and leave with aqua net bangs and curls that reached sky high. The difference was jarring, especially if she also had to do a dye job, our entire apartment reeking with the scent of peroxide or ammonia that made my eyes sting. On those days I was forced to do my homework on the concrete balcony, watching the sea hawks dive close by, hoping for scraps of food.

Now the balcony door was closed and I wondered what I'd see out there at this time, now that the dishes were finished, and the kitchen was gleaming, or as gleaming as you could get with its institutional set-up. It was strange how our lives were supposed to be so much better now that we lived on the American base. The only thing that had really changed was that we traded our rickety, wooden, but character-filled old flat in "the Honch" for living in a high-rise concrete building that reminded me of a prison.

"Come on, it's bed time." I said to Rocky. My ghosts appeared on the other side of the balcony door. They never wanted to hang around when it was dish time. They floated through the glass and I pulled the curtains closed, the yellow porchlight still winking in the darkness. The clock on the wall showed it was 1:00am. At least we'd finished so Mom wouldn't wake me up in the middle of the night.

Rocky trotted off to his room, stopped and looked at me. I knew that look. I passed my parent's room, the stench of alcohol still looming. I closed their door firmly, hoping they were too inebriated to hear it. Rocky grabbed extra blankets and his pillow and dragged them onto the floor of my room.

"The light, Annabelle," he insisted.

I turned on the night light that glowed from pink to blue, to yellow and back again. He turned over to face it and I knew in that moment, his round face glowing with the light, that I couldn't leave him home alone again. I didn't know what Jake would say tomorrow, but maybe if I made Rocky a good breakfast he'd be calm enough for a few hours of strolling.

A thought floated over me as I drifted off to sleep: Mikasa Park. It was Rocky's favourite. Especially the old ship there. I closed my eyes as my ghosts hovered over me, concern on their faces as they circled before settling into a floating sleep themselves.

I waited at the entrance of Sakura tower, its awning covering me from the drizzle of rain that meant I'd likely need a better umbrella. I held one of the cheap, plastic 300 yen ones that my mom always kept stashed in the apartment. If Jake didn't arrive soon, she'd come downstairs to make me sort out her Avon collection or hair accoutrements. I didn't mind, if it meant she'd actually look after Rocky and make sure he got some help. He still couldn't read and all the cultural shame in Japan associated with kids who weren't absolutely "normal" meant that there was a tendency to ignore things I was certain a qualified somebody could help with. I just didn't know who and no one at Rocky's school wanted to talk to his fourteen-year-old sister.

Mom was convinced he was fine, he just needed to "grow up." Duke was certain that "tough love" was the key. His version of tough love consisted of yelling at Rocky until he did things exactly as he said, his southern accent making him almost completely incomprehensible to both of us.

I heard heavy breathing behind me as Rocky rounded the corner, his footsteps echoing on the blue tiled floor of the tower's entranceway. "I come, I come. Don' leave without me!" he yelled.

"He hasn't come yet," I said, taking one of the umbrellas he'd brought. When he wanted to be resourceful, he was fairly helpful. I checked over the edges and it only had one busted side, which meant I likely only had to buy one more umbrella out of the 1,500 yen we had left.

"We have leave before rain. I hate walk in dat rain," he whined.

"That rain" I corrected him.

"Same, same." He sounded just like my mom.

I saw a figure approaching the circular drive with a pink umbrella. He was wearing sandals, cut-off shorts and a white shirt that clung a little too tightly to his thin frame.

"Jake?" I called out and Rocky barrelled toward him. If it wasn't Jake, that guy was going to be in for a surprise.

"Whoa there, Rocky. Slow down." Jake said, beaming up at me and putting his hand out to test the misty air before closing his umbrella. "Sorry I'm late. The people I'm staying with had a fight and the kids were scared. So, I wanted to wait for things to calm down before leaving. At least one of the kids knew where I was going."

"Other kids?" Rocky piped up.

Jake had a look on his face, like a question where he was looking only at me. Almost like permission.

"Some other time Rocky, you're stuck with the two of us today." I said, taking his hand. I wondered when he would be too old for that.

Jake nodded and looked relieved. He whispered in my ear. "I don't think Rocky wants to hang with those two little girls. They make him look like he's ready for sainthood."

I couldn't help laughing. "That's saying something." I pointed with the umbrella toward the route to the closest exit gate and we walked on the slick pavement, the rain still misting around us, but a pleasant change from the scorching day before. The rain made Jake's green eyes darker and sombre. He looked around at the change in scenery, when we cut through the smaller gate guarded by a solitary pair of Marines, passing into the back alleys of Yokosuka.

"How do you know where to go?" Jake

asked, as we wove our way past a few blue tin shacks and noisy pachinko parlours.

"I've lived here my whole life, I don't know anything different."

"But, there are no street signs," he said.

I looked up, wondering what street signs there would be other than the blue highway and main road signs. "I don't think we need them."

He pointed upward, "What if you need to give someone directions?"

I looked around at the different landmarks that told me where to go, my feet automatically knowing without my having to think too deeply about it, unless I was walking past Chuo station to the north of where we were. "I draw them a map."

He seemed satisfied and inhaled deeply, the city chugging along around us, the noodle man out early and singing his short ditty. A few little girls flitted by from the local *yochien*, their blue and white uniforms fluttering in the misty rain as they all donned canary yellow caps.

Jake watched them stare at us as we went by, a few pointing and mouths agape as they heard us speak in English.

Rocky stopped, pointed back and said in growly Japanese "What the heck are you looking at?" The little girls scattered and I pulled him by the arm to the gates of the park.

Rocky clapped his hands and twirled as he skipped over the small fountains flowing along the white tiled walkways leading to

Mikasa park. It was only a matter of time before Rocky shot off and fluttered about, inspecting all of the different fountains. A ginko leaf make its way down the waterway leading into the main park, Rocky charging off ahead with it.

"Do you want me to go get him?" Jake asked.

It wasn't any use running after Rocky. Mikasa Park was easy to find him in. He always ended up in front of the archway, eventually.

"No." I said, feeling shy and not entirely certain why. Jake took my hand and Widow and Koji appeared on either side of us.

"Are you staying?" Koji asked him in Japanese and Jake looked at me, like he couldn't quite discern if he'd heard something or not.

"Is that the little boy ghost?" He asked.

"Yes, he's annoying," I replied.

"No... I'm... not!" Koji said, his English slow and laborious.

Jake watched him flutter off after Rocky. It was funny how Koji never said how he died, how sometimes he acted like he was still alive, maybe even more than Rocky, whose gaze never met mine.

"Come on, there's so much to see," I said, tugging Jake ahead to the main park where the water show had already begun. In the morning light, with only a few visitors, it looked so pristine and almost sanguine. I had taken refuge here more times than I could count, especially once we moved onto the base. At night, before the gates locked, and even sometimes thereafter, teenagers sat drinking *Chu-hi* and sipping soba noodles or meat buns from the local Sunkus. Their cackles and heckling were always alcohol induced. I knew enough of that from my own father to take none of their comments about me seriously. Especially the ones about my two-toned "husky dog" eyes. I'd sit apart from them and watch the water show, feeling that I was maybe a part of their world in those moments. That the dark could hide what made me different from them.

Jake held my hand more firmly as we made our way to the edge of the amphitheatre and three girls in sailor uniforms from my old middle school spotted us. Two pointed and one batted their hands away. Jake looked at me and back to them. An unspoken thought crossing his face. Like he'd known similar mistreatment.

"Is Rocky anywhere nearby?" I asked, breaking hold of his hand while I scanned the ship and surrounding walkways.

"I don't see him, why?" Jake's eyes narrowed as the girls came closer.

Their pleated dark blue skirts swished, their shoes making a familiar rat-tat on the stone steps as they came closer. Yui-chan with her chin-length bob had a look of complete disgust on her face until she was within arm's length of Jake.

"This your boyfriend?" Yui asked me in Japanese.

"I don't know why you care," I replied, crossing my arms.

"Tell them to go away," Jake said. "How do I say that?" He stared Yui-chan down and her two friends cowered, but she stood her ground.

"I can give you what a half-breed never can," she said, her hands on her hips. She licked one bottom lip and then another.

Rocky, with the worst timing ever, stormed toward us, my two ghosts streaming behind him. So, they'd been keeping watch over him, after all.

Koji looked at Yui with a look of rapture on his face. "You...are...disgusting." He buzzed through her hair, producing only the slightest of breezes, and Yui batted at her ears.

Jake started laughing and Widow made water squeeze out of the corner of her kimono and onto Yui's lieutenant's heads. They ran away, screaming curses and profanities at me, the rest of the park staring at them like they were crazy.

"Wait, could they see the ghosts too?" Jake asked, still laughing.

"I don't think so. Not even Rocky can see them," I said.

"Yes, I can." He insisted. But, he thought he'd seen Santa Klaus too and that was as impossible as our birth father coming home to bring us back with him to South Korea, where he'd apparently defected.

"You're the only person I know who can see them," I whispered. Rocky huffed off, annoyed that I didn't believe him, my ghosts trailing him once again, looking very satisfied with themselves.

A stiff breeze brought my long, dark hair around my face. Jake peeled the strands away and looked down at me with those intense green eyes that almost glowed from freckled face. I wanted him to hold me, but I didn't know how to ask.

And in that moment I took a chance—albeit a large one—and threw my arms around his neck, a few tears spilling down my face and onto his white t-shirt that looked like it had been ironed. The scent of dryer sheet still clung to the fabric.

"Oh, Ana. I hate those girls," he said, holding me.

"Me too," I said. "More than you can know."

"If I see them again, I'll hold them down so you can punch them in the gut."

An understanding passed between us as the water show started again, its tinny, canned music sounding very stupid, but the rising water feeling like it was washing away things I had never been able to say, didn't have names for in either of the languages I spoke. In his face, that open understanding meant so much.

I took his arm as we walked through the rest of the water show, on to the peace arch that glinted and cast rainbows on the ground and over the sea stretching out in front of us to the other side of the naval base staring back at us. I liked being on this side of the dark waters, knowing that there was a separation between my new and old life, however tenuous, and the sea and my ghosts were the only things able to bridge it.

I looked up at Jake, wanting to feel his body closer to mine, but unable to know how to ask, why I needed him so desperately in that moment. He looked down at me.

"What is it?" He asked.

The ghosts whooshed in front of us, laughing and carrying on in rapid-fire Japanese that was hard to understand.

CHAPTER THREE

The next morning Rocky silently scrubbed the mountain of dishes that seemed impossible for two people to have used in the hours we'd been gone. Taped to the fridge was another 2,000 yen. Where it came from, I had no idea. I heard a soft knock at the door and Widow floated out and back in. She rarely cared who was at the door. A small smile played at the corner of her mouth.

"It Jake," she whispered in English, then floated next to Rocky, who was oblivious to her, despite his protestations he could see her.

I stood by my parent's bedroom door for a moment, closing it softly, even though my mom would likely get mad about it later. "You don't let boy in our home with my door closed. No closed doors with boys. Ever."

Like I didn't know what happened between boys and girls. Did she think she'd raised me in a nunnery? I didn't want to imagine what she thought, because any chance that I was going to think like her meant I'd also become her, and I didn't want that at all. The concrete was freezing under my feet as I made my way to the front door, its metallic casing rattling a bit as I squeaked it open, Jake tip toeing in, leaving his shoes on the doorstep. We didn't have a proper *genkan*, so I grabbed them and brought them in with him. I'd learned the hard away about how Americans in our tower either stole your shoes or peed in them.

"Morning," he said huskily, leaning down to kiss my cheek. His lips were soft and warm on my skin. I wanted him to do it again.

I looked nervously in the kitchen to Rocky who was soaping up the dishes, attempting to scrub while Koji instructed him in Japanese. Occasionally Rocky nodded his head.

"Does he understand Koji?" Jake asked.

"He can't even hear or see him, though he likes to pretend," I said smiling. I wanted to kiss him back, but I didn't know how to get close enough without feeling awkward. Another missed moment that I wasn't sure how to recover.

"I can help you finish up here so we can leave," Jake pointed to the dishes. The steel counters were almost full and we'd have to dry what was out already before attempting to tackle the rest in the sink.

"I'm not going to say no, but we have to be very quiet. If she sees you here, she'll spaz."

Jake nodded knowingly, then a whisper of a shadow passed across his face. Like a moment from his time before with his Mom coming back to him.

"You thinking about her?" I asked.

"Yeah," he ran his hands through his hair, a lock fell in front of his eyes. I reached up to move the last bit of hair out of his face and he took my hand instead and kissed it before he followed me into the kitchen.

"I saw dat," Rocky said pointing at both of us with soapy fingers. "No kissy, kissy in dis kitchen." He pointed his finger guns at us and we pretended to fall.

"Finish the dishes," Widow whispered. We got stuck in, Koji sing-whispering a song that was old and sad. Outside the dew of rain had stopped and after several minutes of having Jake there, Rocky seemed to get a lift in his spirits that made me less inclined to leave him behind. Besides, who was going to make sure he didn't eat nothing but rainbow puffs all day?

I HELD ROCKY'S PALM TIGHTLY IN MY RIGHT hand, his backpack straps buckled so that I could grab him if he tried to dart out in the crowd. Thankfully, he'd worn his red Super Mario Brother's shirt and rainbow suspenders, so it wouldn't be that difficult to find him, if I needed to. Jake's hand remained on my shoulder as the crowd pressed in on us. I wrapped my hand around his waist, our little trio forced out of Shibuya station and into the massive cross walk with traffic halted for the mass of people making their way out of the station.

"There are so many people," Jake said, as everyone swam around us purposefully, eyes down, a sea of seemingly uniformly dark heads and eyes.

Occasionally someone would look up, make brief eye contact and see my mis-matched eyes before looking away. Rocky was young enough to be spared such looks.

"Tower Records! Tower Records!" Rocky cried. It was the one place he could be still for hours. It probably helped that they had so many listening stations.

Jake laughed and patted Rocky on the back, once we'd crossed the street. "Hey, buddy can't we go to the bakery first?"

Rocky looked at the alleyways before us, knowing the way. Koji followed behind him, but Widow stuck with us, her pink kimono fluttering in the breeze. Couldn't she pick an-other day to be nosy?

As we headed into the bakery, sans Rocky, who was no doubt either stranded in the al-leyway or inside Tower Records already, I spotted his favourite dessert, pan chocolate. I felt Jake's gaze on my face and looked up to see him staring at my lips. He leaned down, his lips briefly touching mine.

So that's how it was.

So fast, so soft.

"I hope that was okay," he said.

"Oh...yes." I said, trying to appear calm and

not as if everything in me was alight with a new energy.

The bakery attendants stared at us blankly, like they'd never seen two people kiss. Then they started to giggle. I brought his face close to mine again and kissed him, letting my tongue taste the saltiness of his lips.

"I don't know if I need any more sweets," Jake teased.

I poked him in the ribs and kept my arm around his waist as we made our way to the counter.

THE COVER OF THE TAPE JAKE HELD DISPLAYED American guys with spikey hair at the front and shaggy at the sides.

"Survivor is the best," Jake said, putting the earphones over me. I searched behind us for Rocky, who was jamming out to Michael Jackson. The important thing was that he was occupied, which meant I might be able to enjoy this moment, surrounded by rows of tapes and records, the rows just high enough and the curve of the counter solid enough for me to move closer to Jake.

When Survivor's lead singer harmonized with the guitarist, their voices blended as they sang about searching the whole world to find this girl. Jake leaned in.

"Can you hear it?" I asked him.

"Of course. I know every word to this song, backwards and forwards." He took me into his arms and I slid the earphones off, turning up the volume and hanging them up on the hook. I reached my arms up high over his neck as he wrapped his hands around my waist, tentatively, like he wasn't sure if that was okay.

I looked up and his mouth was on mine, tipping me gently against the tape racks, his body harder against mine. I felt a supreme calm and then a searing heat flashing through me as his tongue gently touched mine.

The song finished and I let go of him. Knowing that we had crossed a line. A shopkeeper stared at us angrily and it was obvious we had to buy something or leave.

Jake's cheeks were flushed. He put a hand on my cheek. "I'm sorry if I went too far...I care about you...I don't want to ruin...this." He took my hand tentatively. He looked over at the glaring shopkeeper. "I don't want to do anything wrong."

I could not feel more full of him than at any other time. The words of a million unsung songs flooded through my hijacked mind. The song played again and I pointed to the rack of tapes. "Let's get this Survivor album."

He was looking at me like he wasn't going to budge without my acknowledging what had happened. It was strange how old he looked then. My ghosts floating above us, their expressions a bit embarrassed. Had they seen everything?

"You didn't do anything wrong, Jake. I want to be with you. Please don't worry." And in that moment my head was saying, Iloveyou, I-love-you, I love...youuuuuu, in at least three different languages. How could I love someone I had only just met? And was that even possible for someone like me, who even bullies had feared to touch?

My burnished brown hair, straight and shiny rushed into my face from my collapsed ponytail and I let it fall, no longer wishing to always have it together when that didn't seem possible anymore.

"Let's get that tape then." Jake said, his arm around my waist, the shopkeeper scowling at us, even after we'd paid and collected Rocky. My ghosts whisked through him and he blinked as though he'd been fleeced.

CHAPTER FOUR

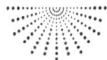

The next afternoon, Jake took my hand and I struggled to keep up with his long stride. The sun was burning above us and I wished I'd brought my hat, but that would mean that I was letting my mother win about the perils of having dark skin. We reached a high concrete barrier and he took me by the waist, lifting me over. My thigh caught on some loose barbed wire and I felt a tear on the side my thigh and a searing pain where rivulets of blood fell.

"Ooh, you're bleeding," he said.

I wiped at it and smeared the blood my frayed dark jean shorts. "I'll be fine, it only stings." I didn't want to be that Japanese schoolgirl who couldn't handle blood. I needed him to see me as strong and capable, even if no one else in my life seemed to treat me that way, except Rocky.

Widow and Koji had disappeared that morning. We walked among the rubble of the landfill, the soil spongey under my feet, a stri-

ated mixture of sand, soil, rocks and other debris that had been flung into the landfill to
extend the borders of the base.

"Why do they do this?" Jake asked. "It looks
like a wasteland."

"Japan doesn't have enough flat land so
they fill in areas like this one and when so
many years have gone by, they build things
on it."

Jake looked at me, his face wide in disbe-
lief. "Did this use to be ocean?"

"I think so, but I only moved to the base a
year ago. We'd better hop over the other side
before we get caught," I saw a patrol car in the
distance, making its way around the hill to the
left.

Jake pointed toward the hill, "that's where
we're headed." He had a sure grin on his face.
As soon as we reached the opposite side of the
concrete landfill enclosure, the soil wet under
our feet, he lifted me into the air again and this
time waited until I'd cleared the last of the
barbed wire.

There was a care, a gentleness to his touch.
It wasn't like the guys from my old school
trying to look up girl's skirts or touch their
barely-there breasts. There was none of that
hunger in his eyes. None of that urging to
push me where I wasn't ready. I wondered if,
in this secluded spot that was all going to
change?

I followed him up the well-trimmed grass,
the steep hill at a much higher incline than I'd
expected. I was panting by the time we got to

the top, the grass growing in even, thin green strands. It looked like it needed watering, but I knew it was a matter of time before the summer rains arrived. They were never far away.

The sky was a deep cornflower blue punctuated by thick clouds swiftly traveling by. At this height, with a larger ridge of hillside and thick foliage growing behind us, it felt like I was on the top of the world with only the sky between me and outer space. It was incredibly freeing, but also dizzying and I plopped down on the grass. The cicadas started up again with their buzzing, protesting the heat more loudly than usual.

Jake approached tentatively, removing his shoes and turning on his side to gaze at me before watching the hawks chasing each other above us. "One of those birds stole my Dad's hamburger out of his mouth once."

"Yeah, they can do that. But they have to be incredibly hungry." I laughed thinking about Enoshima and how my brother had liked to throw bits of buns into the air for the hawks.

Jake's hand was outstretched toward me, asking for something I wasn't sure of. I took his hand and he moved closer, looking nervous. I pulled him closer to me, so his body folded into mine, a perfect S-curve of two bodies, his head on my chest.

"I can hear your heartbeat, Annabelle. What is it saying?" He asked.

I could hear the thuds too and I knew what they were saying, but I didn't want to let him in yet. I needed this moment to be what it was and not something more, because I didn't have the right words for all the feelings. I needed time to think, to imagine all the ways my words could go wrong before I said them.

"*Himitsu.*" I replied.

"What's that?"

"Secret," I said.

"Girls always have secrets." He whispered, kissing the top of my head. He leaned over me, his face flushed, kissing me and bringing me to sit up before I pushed him back on the grass, my body on his, my dark hair forming a curtain over him and me. I laid there on him, our legs entwined and kissed him back.

I turned on my side when I felt him move under me, that gentle shifting telling me we had gone far enough, his hand on my waist as he looked up at the hawks circling above.

"I'm calling it Mt. Fuji," he said.

"But it isn't."

"I know, it's somewhere over there." He pointed in the right direction of the Tokyo Wan.

"On a clear day you can see it, especially after a typhoon," I said.

"Someday, we'll climb it and we'll be free of all of them: annoying guardians, weird parents…bullies." He spoke with an assurance that made me believe that my life wouldn't always be like this, that his presence had the ability to transport me beyond Yokosuka to a world that might welcome me on equal terms.

I laid back against him, hands entwined.

"I'd like that." There was so much more I could say, but something deep and visceral held me back. Like the tide to my emotions had to be let loose in a way I didn't understand.

"For now, this is our Mt. Fuji," I declared, bringing his hand to my heart.

"Our new meeting place," he agreed, kissing my hand.

CHAPTER FIVE

The next day he didn't show up at "Mt. Fuji." After an hour of waiting, I looked for him in all the residential towers, the pools, even checking the bowling alley while the pins rolled listlessly back, their empty sound taunting me. After a cursory search, I ran outside before anyone saw my tears. I circled back to the apartment where he was staying, knocking on the door while feet shuffled in the background and a child wailed. I knocked again and counted to fifty before leaving, my body shaking without me understanding why.

The second day I sat by the front gate with Rocky for several hours, even combing the bike racks for his bicycle. We tried his tower again, this time avoiding the urine stench of the elevator to climb the stairs to the fifth floor, knocking on the door, Rocky's ear pressed to it. My ghosts floated inside and floated back, looking despondent.

I knocked again. The family he was staying with had to tell me something. Rocky banged loudly on the metal door, Koji and Widow scattering away from us.

The door creaked open, a withered looking pale women stepping out in her nightgown. "What do you want?" She smelled of sour milk.

"I'm worried about Jake."

"He's long gone, honey. Go away," she rasped and closed the door before I could ask anything else.

ON THE THIRD AFTERNOON OF MY SEARCH, I climbed to the top of our grassy hill, thick grey clouds rolling in. Maybe if I waited here, I'd know. Widow and Koji were my silent companions. I closed my eyes and kept seeing his face. When I opened them, the slate sea was wild below. Widow and Koji levitated in the air directly above me. "Why can't you tell me where he is?"

"We do not know," they said in unison.

The wind picked up and blew my hair around my face, which I had no doubt had a horrible scowl plastered on it.

"Annabelle?" a voice called out for me faintly. I wasn't sure if it was the wind tricking me.

I crouched over the hill to see who it was, hoping by some miracle it was him.

Rocky's squat figure hadn't yet looked up. He was collecting beetles at the bottom.

I rolled over to the other side of the hill, the grass scratching at the back of my neck. Rocky kept calling out for me, but I didn't want to be found. I gingerly made my way toward the sea wall on the opposite side of the hill, hopping over the waist-high barrier and onto the gigantic concrete jacks that led down to the swells.

The charm bracelet Jake had given me tinkled in the wind. I picked up smooth stones that had been left on the tops of the jacks and tossed one after the other into the ocean, the swells too large to see where my rocks had sunk beneath the depths. The grey, snarling beast of the sea looked like it was ready to devour everything in sight. It was the worst I had ever seen it, except right before a typhoon.

I knew I had to head inside, but being near the last place I'd seen him linked me to his disappearance. It helped me feel that he must've gone for reasons that were very personal, very sad, yet incomprehensible to me.

I didn't know what love was then. I wasn't certain how this could be romance, because it felt like something deeper than what I read in my manga, something more drawn out than movies I'd watched with my mother while she permed women's hair, or anything resembling what she'd had with the two men I'd watch her burn through.

I wondered if I was destined for her fate, even with my two-toned eyes and darker skin. When I stopped being what people wanted, expected me to be as the dutiful, ever-suffering older daughter, would their love run cold too?

That couldn't apply to Jake, I thought. I

threw another stone over the seawall, crawling to the top and letting the spray hit my face, almost willing the waves to crash over me and strip me clean from the grief that was gnawing away at all of the joy that had been there days before.

Could I just forget the nights imagining Jake holding me, though he never did anything more than hold my hand and kiss me? That touch had more gravity than anything anyone else had done for me. And now, to have to go back to the reality I'd been in before was unbearable.

The waves roared upwards, their green-grey swells getting taller and taller. I felt a touch on the back of my neck. Widow was waiting there, *"Abunai."* She was beckoning me back to safety.

I nodded once and climbed down. She was right. It didn't make sense to let my fourteen-year old body get dashed to pieces on the seawall just because of one disappearing boy.

I trudged back up the hill.

The ghosts hovered there, not a welcome presence or companionship, but a weight pressing on me. Koji bounced thoughtfully, his eyes darting around my face. Widow with her mouth pressed in a thin line. "No good comes from mourning a man, just look at me."

Finally, Koji exhaled loudly and slumped beside me, his icy fingers going through me again and again before he curled up on the grass, like a cat. "She's right, you know," he yawn-spoke before falling asleep.

I wanted them to vanish forever, if it meant having Jake back for a few minutes.

To know that I hadn't imagined him.

Three days ago, I had decided I was going to tell him: what was fluttering behind the chambers of my heart, rushing through my veins, so deep inside me that no language had the syntax to elucidate what was written under my skin. And yet I was ready to let that current of feeling try to come out in words. Hopefully English ones he could understand. I'd waited too long and lost my chance.

"You'll always have us," Koji said.

"We'll never go away." Widow said with a wide-eyed look that was attempting to be hopeful.

I remembered Jake's large hand in mine and I stretched back and watched the brown wings of the sea hawks circle above my head, recalling the tension in his shoulders as we soared through the streets of Kamakura only days ago. The sea hawks swooped closer and I rose to stand on top of the hill, the whitecaps on the ocean growing more furious. I spread my arms and the hawks scattered, crying to each other.

My ghosts were all that remained.

WWW.BRITTAJENSEN.COM

DID YOU ENJOY GHOSTS OF YOKOSUKA?

A few sentences on Amazon or
Goodreads help a lot!
E-mail us at murasakipress at
gmail dot com with your published
review and join our VIP list as
thanks for your time!

PLEASE WRITE A BOOK REVIEW!

JOIN THE AUTHOR'S MAILING LIST:

www.brittajensen.com

ACKNOWLEDGMENTS

This book is made possible because of the generosity of patrons: W.D Summitt, J. Hansen, A. Reader, A. Bailey and Y. Willhoite. I'm especially grateful for feedback from Adam Marek, John Pipkin, classmates in the WLT Advanced Fiction class, Faber Academy classmates, Kara Stockinger, Roanna Flowers, Annie Williams, Gina Springer Shirley + Women Writer's Group, and for crucial final stage edits from A.R. Bennett, Maggie Gentry, Farha Quadri, Aye-Tee Monaco and Peter Iannucci. Heartfelt thanks to many early readers & support from Jen Denison, PJ Hoover and Bill Cotter. This story wouldn't be possible without my parents, who brought me to Yokosuka, Japan in 1989 and made certain our family stayed there as long as possible. I'm grateful for those twelve amazing years and the *natsukashi* moments.

There are a lot of elements in this story that may seem odd to non-residents of Yokosuka,

Japan in 1985. It was a city in transition and, like many post-war cities, it was altered by the allied bombings. Rebuilding the city took a lot longer than anyone anticipated. Within this port city, its economy tied to the US Navy's presence, there was a mix of cultures: Japanese, Filipino, Korean, American, Russian, etc.

Children who were in-between cultures, born on the Japanese economy, like Annabelle was, were often treated with disparagement in these close-knit communities. Thus, when friendships on the military base were made between outsiders, they were fast-moving because life on a military community required quick bonds in order for the community to survive. As a result, those unfamiliar with this way of life might find the friendship between Jake and Annabelle to be a bit odd, but for those who lived this fast-paced, frenetic and nomadic existence, it will feel very normal. I've had to take liberties with certain historical and cultural details for the sake of the story's integrity. I hope the reader will be generous with my interpretation of my beloved hometown and its many wandering spirits.

ABOUT THE AUTHOR

 Britta Jensen's debut novel, *Eloia Born* won the Writer's League of Texas 2019 YA Discovery Prize. It's sequel, *Hirana's War* released in 2020. Her short stories have been short-listed for several prizes in the UK. After living overseas in Japan, South Korea and Germany for twenty-two years, her multi-lingual, cross-cultural heritage influences her writing in myriad ways.

She now lives in Austin, TX where she is working on her next YA novel, *Orphan Pods*. Britta has taught writing to adults & teens for the past seventeen years, edits books with The Writing Consultancy and Yellowbird Editors, and teaches writing at St Edwards University.

Get free writing advice by joining her mailing list and access bonus content on her website www.brittajensen.com. She loves hearing from readers!

patreon.com/brittajensenwrites

youtube.com/UCiUt34gZPUDT9c-Om2s2D90A

goodreads.com/7731330.Britta_Jensen

www.ingramcontent.com/pod-product-compliance
Lightning Source LLC
Chambersburg PA
CBHW020347110726
47898CB00003B/1072